A catalogue record for this book is available from the British Library

Published by Ladybird Books Ltd Loughborough Leicestershire UK
Ladybird Books Ltd is a subsidiary of the Penguin Group of companies
Text © Tony Bradman MCMXCVI
© LADYBIRD BOOKS LTD MCMXCVI
LADYBIRD and the device of a Ladybird are trademarks of Ladybird Books Ltd

What's wrong with Bertie?

by Tony Bradman
illustrated by Peter Stevenson

Bertie was a very clever little bunny. He could write the most amazing stories. He could draw the most fantastic pictures. And he could sing the most wonderful songs. All Bertie needed was some peace and quiet.

But Bertie the bunny had *fourteen* brothers and sisters. So peace and quiet was something Bertie *never* got. Whenever he thought he was alone, along would come...

Boris and Betty and Billy and Belle, and Barry and
Brenda and Brian as well, and Bobby and Bradley
and Beattie and… yes, Barney and Beryl and
Barbara and Bess. And they soon spoilt everything.

"Hey, Bertie!" they would say, bouncing up and
down. "Tell us a story! Draw us a picture! Sing us a
song! *Please*, Bertie. You're brilliant!"

"Oh, all right," Bertie would say.

Bertie loved his brothers and sisters. But he was fed up. He *had* to get some peace and quiet, or he would go bonkers. Then one day, Bertie had an idea. He decided to try hiding from them.

"They'll never find me by the hedge at the edge of the meadow..." he thought, and smiled to himself.

Bertie bided his time... then sneaked out of the bunny hole, and hoppity-hopped across the meadow as fast as he could go.

For a few delicious moments he was alone. It was
very peaceful and quiet. Bertie watched the
frantic ants, he listened to the buzzy bees, and he
sniffed the sweet-smelling flowers. But then
along came…

Boris and Betty and Billy and Belle, and Barry and Brenda and Brian as well, and Bobby and Bradley and Beattie and… yes, Barney and Beryl and Barbara and Bess. And they soon spoilt everything.

"Hey, Bertie!" they said, bouncing up and down. "What are you doing? Bet it's something *really* exciting. Can we play?"

"No, you can't," said Bertie, crossly. Then he hoppity-hopped back to the bunny hole, muttering all the way.

That evening, Bertie was a very grumpy bunny.

"What's wrong with Bertie?" everybody wanted to know.

The next day, Bertie decided to try hiding outside again.

"They'll never find me by the bank of the rippling river," he thought, and smiled to himself.

Bertie bided his time… then sneaked out of the bunny hole and hoppity-hopped to the bank of the river as fast as he could go.

For a few delicious moments he was alone. It was very peaceful and quiet. He watched the fish swishing, he listened to the croaky frogs, and he sniffed the rich muddy smell of the river. But then along came…

Boris and Betty and Billy and Belle, and Barry and Brenda and Brian as well, and Bobby and Bradley and Beattie and... yes, Barney and Beryl and Barbara and Bess. And they soon spoilt everything.

"Hey, Bertie!" they said, bouncing up and down. "There you are! For a while we thought you were actually hiding from us!"

"What gave you *that* idea?" said Bertie, crossly. Then he hoppity-hopped back to the bunny hole, muttering all the way.

That evening, Bertie was a very grumpy bunny indeed. In fact, he was so grumpy, he even shouted… *at his teddy bear!*

"What's wrong with Bertie?" everybody whispered.

He went in beneath the trees, where it was *very* peaceful and *very* quiet. He was truly, deliciously… alone at last.

Bertie watched a seed pod twirling and whirling down to the ground, he listened to the birds twittering, he sniffed the leaves, and felt the gentle evening breeze.

Bertie thought of amazing new stories to write, fantastic new pictures to draw, and wonderful new songs to sing. But there was something missing… Bertie had no one to share them with. Besides, the sun was setting and the darkness was creeping slowly towards Bertie. An owl hooted, and there was a howling in the distance…

Suddenly, Bertie heard a rustling in the bushes. It got nearer, and nearer, and nearer. Bertie trembled with fear. Then along came…

That evening, Bertie was a very... *cheerful*
bunny. After all, he had no reason for gloom.
Not now that he had his own little... *room*!
And who do you think were his very first guests?

That's right!

Boris and Betty and Billy and Belle, and Barry and
Brenda and Brian as well, and Bobby and Bradley
and Beattie and... yes, Barney and Beryl and
Barbara and Bess.

Boris

Billy

Belle

Betty

Picture Ladybird

Books for reading aloud with 2 – 6 year olds

The exciting *Picture Ladybird* series includes a wide range
of animal stories, funny rhymes, and real life adventures that are
perfect to read aloud and share at storytime or bedtime.

A whole library of beautiful books for you to collect

RHYMING STORIES

Easy to follow and great for joining in!

Jasper's Jungle Journey, Val Biro
Shoo Fly, Shoo! Brian Moses
Ten Tall Giraffes, Brian Moses
In Comes the Tide, Valerie King
Toot! Learns to Fly,
Geraldine Taylor & Jill Harker
Who Am I? Judith Nicholls
Fly Eagle, Fly! Jan Pollard

IMAGINATIVE TALES

Mysterious and magical, or just a little shivery

The Star that Fell, Karen Hayles
Wishing Moon, Lesley Harker
Don't Worry William, Christine Morton
This Way Little Badger, Phil McMylor
The Giant Walks, Judith Nicholls
Kelly and the Mermaid, Karen King

FUNNY STORIES

Make storytime good fun!

Benedict Goes to the Beach, Chris Demarest
Bella and Gertie, Geraldine Taylor
Edward Goes Exploring, David Pace
Telephone Ted, Joan Stimson
Top Shelf Ted, Joan Stimson
Helpful Henry, Shen Roddie
What's Wrong with Bertie? Tony Bradman
Bears Can't Fly, Val Biro
Finnigan's Flap, Joan Stimson

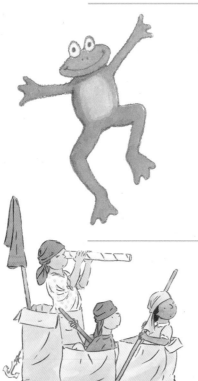

REAL LIFE ADVENTURE

Situations to explore and discover

Joe and the Farm Goose,
Geraldine Taylor & Jill Harker
Going to Playgroup,
Geraldine Taylor & Jill Harker
The Great Rabbit Race, Geraldine Taylor
Pushchair Polly, Tony Bradman